AF580621

Turtleberry Press

Baltimore, MD 21234

www.turtleberrypress.com

Ayanna is a stressed-out school counselor and ready for Spring Break. Then her boyfriend decides they need to take a break to reevaluate their relationship. She posts her frustration on social media. Then Zack, an old flame, slides into her DMs. He offers to help her enjoy her break.

“I just think we should take a break to think about where things are going with us.” Mike had his back to me as he sat at the foot of the bed.

I still stared at him. I knew he could feel me staring at the back of his head but he didn’t turn around. The post-sex haze had completely faded away and, when I was tired of staring at the back of Mike’s head, I looked around for my clothes.

“Are you going to say something?” Mike spoke without turning around.

I got up and started to get dressed. “Okay.”

“That’s it?” He finally turned and looked at me.

I decided I didn’t want to look at him anymore so I got dressed with my back to him. “Yup.”

“We’ve been together for over a year and I just want to make sure we are moving in the right direction. A break would be good so we can clear our heads and...”

“I said okay.” I snapped. I really hoped he didn’t open his mouth again. A headache was forming and I wanted to get home to two Aleve and a glass of wine.

“Ayanna...” Mike stood up.

I pulled my shirt on and walked out of his bedroom. My shoes, jacket, and purse were in the living room of his apartment. By the time I got my shoes on, Mike was standing there looking at me. He was still naked. He was a good-looking man. But the site that had gotten me excited only two hours earlier now made my head throb. I quickly thought about anything I might have left in his apartment that I would not want to have to replace. All I could remember was having toiletries in his bathroom. We had just gotten to that point.

We weren't even at the point where I was leaving clothes.

"Ayanna, don't go. I want to talk about this."

I cut my eyes at him, grabbed my coat and purse, and left out the door.

How do I change my relationship status to "On A Break"? Asking for an annoyed me.

I posted the status while taking Aleve when I got home from Mike's place. Then I closed the app on my phone and went to see if I could scrub him off of me. I didn't even think about the status again until my best friend Charmaine called me the next day after work.

“What’s up Char?”

“I meant to call your ass last night but it was late when I saw your post.” She paused. “What’s going on? On a break?”

I sighed. “He said he wanted a break.”

“A break for what?”

“To see if we are on the right track.”

“You need a break for that?” She sucked her teeth. “Old ass fuck boy.”

“Exactly.”

“What did you say?”

“I told him okay and then left.”

“You didn’t entertain a discussion?”

“Naw. I had a headache.”

“Good. That didn’t deserve a discussion. How you forty years old and need a break to figure out what to do with your relationship?”

"Girl, don't get me started to lying."

"Shit is giving me a headache." She paused. "How was work today?"

"Not too bad. No major meltdowns. Regularly scheduled meetings with a few students who all just seemed to be stressed about what high school they are going to."

"Not like last week?"

"No." I shook my head like she could see me. The week before I had three separate students in major crises. With one of them, I had to involve Child Protective Services because of some things that were going on in the home. That was always a tough call to make. It was one of my more stressful weeks as a Middle School Social Worker. One of a series of tough weeks.

"Spring break is soon, right?"

"Two weeks."

"What are you going to do?"

"Relax. Probably sleep and catch up on some reading."

"You should go somewhere and do something fun."

"With who? You're going to be working."

"I dunno. Maybe by yourself." Char paused. "Never mind. I don't like that idea. Doesn't seem safe."

"Exactly."

"We'll go somewhere this summer."

"Sounds nice."

"Your DMs probably look crazy. I can tell it just from the number of guys shooting their shot in response to your post."

"Ugh." I groaned. "Now I gotta weed through all of that."

"Let me know if you get anything interesting."

"I will."

"Talk to you later."

"Later." I disconnected the call and just glanced at my purse in the passenger seat of my car. My phone had been in there all day. I decided to check my mentions and DMs while I ate dinner. Maybe it would be entertaining.

As soon as I got in the house, I kicked off my shoes and headed straight for the kitchen. I turned on some music and started dinner. After surveying my options for a few moments, I threw together some frozen shrimp, frozen vegetables, pasta, and a jar of sauce I had in the cabinet. When it was finished, I fixed a container for lunch the next day and a plate to eat right then. I walked past my dining room table and got comfortable on my couch with my tablet. Took a few bites of my food before I opened up the app to check my mentions and DMs.

Just like Charmaine told me, there were several responses to my status. A few from women who posted in solidarity. Then there were a few guys that made me laugh with their inquiries into my status. I went to my DMs and was pleased to see there were only three new message threads. My eyes immediately skipped over the first two and went to the third. It was from a familiar name. Zachary and I used to have an on-again/off-again situation in college. It went on from sophomore year until I graduated and moved away for graduate school. We were mutuals on a few different social media platforms and occasionally had quick conversations in recent years. I opened his message to see if he was poking fun at me.

Can an old friend get your number?

Under his message was a phone number. I stared at it for a few moments before picking up my phone and typing the number into my text message app.

Me - Hi old friend.

I sat my phone down and went back to my tablet. I checked the other two messages and realized that I should have just skipped over them altogether. One was a very unimpressive, unsolicited dick pic. He got blocked quickly. The other was a guy shooting his shot using language I heard my students using. A bit of investigation helped me learn that he was somewhere in his early twenties. With no intention of being a cougar, I deleted his message. I decided to post a selfie I had taken during my lunch break. Then I heard my phone vibrate on the side table. I picked it up to see a message from Zack.

Zack - YaniBelle

Zack - How are you?

I smiled at him using the nickname he gave me in college when he found out my middle name was Isabel.

Me - I'm good.

Me - How are you?

Zack - Pretty good.

Zack - Especially seeing that picture you just posted

Me - LOL

Zack - You have spring break coming up, right?

Me - Yeah

Zack - Any big plans?

Me - Just to relax and catch up on some reading.

Zack - Come visit me

I had to read his words a few times for them to register in my brain. Then I tried to figure out how to respond. My brain wasn't being helpful in that regard.

Me - Huh?

Zack - Come to Miami and visit me

Zack - I'll buy your ticket

Zack - I have a guest room you can stay in or can get you a hotel room if it makes you more comfortable

Me - Miami is going to be full of kids on break

Zack - I'm not in that part of Miami

Me - We haven't seen each other in forever

Zack - Exactly

I felt like I should be more conflicted than I was. Everything in me was telling me to say yes. There wasn't even a hint of doubt in my mind or any small voice saying that this wasn't a good idea. It was like almost two decades hadn't passed and he was calling me so he could see me. I was just as eager as I had always been.

Me - Don't you have to work?

Zack - I'm the boss. I'll give myself a few days off.

Me - LOL

Me - Must be nice

Zack - So am I buying this ticket?

Me - Yes

"I still can't believe you are going to visit this man." Char looked at me while the nail technician began her pedicure. "Did you decide to get a hotel room?"

"Nope. I'm going to stay at his place."

"Ayanna, you haven't seen this man in forever. What if…"

"He's a serial killer?"

"Yes."

"I don't think he is. We've been talking a lot since we exchanged numbers. He is the same Zack I remember from college."

"It could all be a front." Char paused. "Are you getting the same color on your hands?"

"Yes."

"I like your braids." She reached over and tossed a few braids over my shoulder.

"So, you are going to stop fussing now?"

"I want you to take a picture of his driver's license and the back of his car so I can see his plates. I need his address and all his social media handles."

"I told you who he was on social media."

"I know. I looked. But I want you to type it up in an email. I already know where he works but put that in the email too."

I laughed. "Seriously?"

“Yes. If something happens to you, I have something to give the cops unless you want me to find him and deal with him myself.”

“Nothing is going to happen to me.”

“That’s what the victim always says on those true crime shows.” Char raised an eyebrow. “I’m not playing. I want all that information.”

“Fine.”

“I also want you to have a good time.” She leaned over and spoke softly. “You had the wax appointment?”

I laughed. “Yes.”

“So, you are ready for whatever. Good. I’m proud of you.”

“Thanks.”

“When we leave here, we will go to the mall so you can get some new lingerie for the week.”

"I don't need..."

"Yes, you do."

"If I let him see what I have, it'll be new to him anyway."

"It'll make you feel good." She nodded. "Trust me on this."

"I guess."

"And you said if you let him see like you don't already know you're gonna let him."

"Only if the energy is right."

"Well let us pray for good energy then." Char paused. "Why, again, didn't you two work out years ago?"

"Neither of us was ready to settle down and I moved away for graduate school." I sighed. "We were so young."

"Do you wish you would have tried?"

"No." I said quickly. "Like I said. We were young. I wouldn't change a thing."

“Just make sure you come home. I saw pictures of that man and he is fine. Don’t get any ideas about staying down there. You aren’t allowed to leave me.”

“I’m coming back. I’m just getting away for a few days.”

“A week in Miami with that fine ass man. Don’t get pregnant.”

I burst out laughing.

Zachary was standing in baggage claim wearing a three-piece suit. I had spent the entire flight reminiscing about our relationship and he had the nerve to be standing there looking way more delicious than I remembered. I had to pause because too many feelings came flooding back. My heart reminded me of how much I loved that man and my body reminded me of how much I craved him. He didn’t see me at first so I had a moment to collect myself. I needed to calm myself down so I didn't run over and wrap my body around him. That suit he was wearing was cut perfectly for him. He was bigger than I remembered. Pictures told me that he was no longer the skinny guy from our youth but they honestly didn't do him justice. Zack looked much better in person. I wondered what else about him was bigger because he was clearly a grown-ass man now.

Zack spotted me and a smile slowly formed on his face. My heart skipped a beat as I noticed he still had that one dimple. We slowly walked over to each other. He reached out for my hands when we got close enough.

"You don't post enough full-body pics." He looked me up and down. "You're hiding all this grown woman you got going on."

I smiled. "Trying to cut back on how many admirers I have."

Zack pulled me close. We hugged and he kissed me on the cheek. Then he stepped back and looked me over again. “You look amazing.”

I quickly glanced down at my outfit. I was wearing yoga pants, a t-shirt, a cropped hoodie, and a pair of Chucks. “I feel underdressed.”

Zack chuckled. “I just left a meeting.”

“On a Saturday?”

“On a Saturday.” He nodded and then reached for the bag I was carrying. “One more bag?”

“Yes.” I looked at the belt as the bell sounded and bags began to appear. I pointed out my bag when it came around.

Zack grabbed my suitcase and then freed up one arm so he could wrap it around mine. Then he led the way out to the parking garage. “How was your flight?”

“It was good. Crowded but good.”

“Miami is popular right now.”

“Very.”

Zack stopped at the back of a shiny Range Rover. While he put my suitcase and bag in the back, I thought about what Char asked for. I didn’t need her blowing up my phone or coming down to Miami because I didn’t follow her instructions.

“I’m supposed to take a picture of your car and your license for my best friend.” I paused. “Just in case.”

Zack chuckled and shut the back of the truck. “Make it easier for her to find me if I abduct you?”

“Yes.”

“Want me to pose in the picture?” Zack smiled and pointed to his license plates.

I laughed as I pulled out my phone and took a picture. “Got it.”

He pulled out his wallet and took out his driver's license. "Should I hold it up to my face?"

"No." I playfully swatted at his arm. I took a picture of it when he held it out for me. "Thank you for indulging me. She'll come looking for me if she thinks I'm in danger."

"It's good to have friends like that." He put his license away and then put his wallet back in his pocket. I couldn't help but look at how nice his pants fit. Zack cleared his throat. "Eyes up here."

I let my eyes move up to his face slowly. His smile made me smile. "My bad."

"Come here."

I walked closer to him. Zack ran his finger down my cheek and then kissed me softly on the lips. I loved that we were almost the same height. It was something that I always loved about him. Since he was only 5'10, I could kiss him without him bending down or me craning my neck or standing on my toes. His kiss was just as soft as I remembered it being. He slipped his arms around my waist and pulled me close while parting my lips with his tongue. I almost got lost in the kiss. Then Zack's hands moved to my ass and I started giggling.

Zack stepped back after planting a kiss on my forehead. "Let's get you back to my place so you can start relaxing."

I nodded. Zack stepped closer and kissed me softly on the lips one more time. Then he opened the door and helped me into his truck. I put my seatbelt on and got comfortable for the ride. Zack had always been such a good driver. He was one of the few people I ever fell asleep while riding with. Most people made me nervous. I could have dozed off on the ride to his place if I wasn't so busy looking at the passing scenery. I had only been to Miami once and that was a trip to South Beach back about fifteen years earlier. Everything I saw as we navigated the city was new to me.

"We're here." Zack said as he turned in front of a tall building. It looked new. I didn't get to notice much else before he turned into the parking garage.

After he parked and we got out of his truck, I was too busy watching Zack walk in front of me to pay attention to my surroundings. His ass, as well as the rest of him, looked really good in that suit. I realized that I had never actually seen him in a suit before. He never wore them years ago when we were seeing each other and all of his recent social media posts were of him in casual attire. This was definitely a side of him that I liked a lot.

"Do you wear suits often?" I asked as we stood on opposite sides of the elevator.

"No. You caught me on a day when it was necessary. I'm more of a business casual kind of guy."

"Lucky me." I smiled.

"If you like it, I'll have to wear another one when we go out this week."

"Please and thank you."

Zack winked at me and then led the way off the elevator when the doors opened. His door was all the way down the hall. When he opened the door, I was immediately struck by all the windows. There was an incredible view of the city.

"This is nice." I said after a few moments of staring at the view.

"Let me show you around." Zack left my bags where they were and took my hand. He led me around his condo. He had a gourmet kitchen that made me giggle. He looked at me. "What's funny?"

“Do you cook in here?” I raised an eyebrow. When we were seeing each other, he couldn’t even boil water. I remembered teaching him to make eggs.

“I dabble a little bit.” He smiled. “Not often but I do.”

I nodded and let him lead me through the great room. “You had a designer?”

“I did.”

“They did an amazing job.”

Zack stopped and grabbed my bags before showing me to the guest room. He stood in the doorway after setting my things near the bed. “What do you think?”

“This is nice.” I glanced out the window. “I still can’t get over this view.”

He walked over to the bedside table and picked up a remote. “This is for the blinds.”

“Thanks.”

"Bathroom is through that door." Zack pointed to a door. "I'm on the other side of the apartment."

"You're about to leave me by myself?"

Zack chuckled. "I figured you would want to get settled. I want to get out of this suit. Come get me once you are settled."

I nodded. "Okay."

Once Zack headed down the hallway, I explored the guest suite. The room was a good size and the bathroom was really nice. I sat on the bed for only a few moments before hopping up and opening up my suitcase. The first thing I did was hang up a few things that needed it. Then I grabbed some clothes and my toiletries and headed straight into the bathroom to test out that shower. Even though it was just a couple of hours on the plane, I still felt icky. The water pressure was amazing. I let it massage my back for a bit before I started to wash up. My mind began to wonder if Zack was in the shower. Then I remembered all the showers we had taken together in the past.

Those memories caused me to get out of the shower with an itch I desperately needed Zack to scratch. After putting on lotion, I pulled on my matching pajama shorts and tank top. I wasn't sure what Zack planned but I knew where my mind was. We used to always be on the same page and I hoped that twenty years hadn't changed that. I slipped on my slippers and headed across the condo to the master bedroom.

The door was halfway open so I felt like that meant I could come in. I could hear the shower running in the bathroom so I kicked off my slippers and sat cross-legged on his huge bed. A few moments later, the shower stopped. I pictured him drying off and putting on lotion. I got nervous when the bathroom door opened. Zack's smile, and that dimple, caused my nerves to subside.

"All settled?"

"Sorta."

Zack was wearing nothing but a towel around his waist. He walked into the bedroom and I immediately wondered if his dick had gotten bigger. The way he was walking had me sure that it had. He stood at the edge of the bed. "Come here."

I scooted over to him. "Did you have plans for us?"

"I have a lot of plans for us." Zack traced his finger down my arm and then rested both of his hands on my hips.

"I don't want to mess up your plans."

He kissed me on each of my cheeks and then on the lips. "Trust me. This is part of the plan."

"I like that we are on the same page." I removed the towel from his waist and admired the effect time had on his body.

"When were we ever not on the same page?" He pulled my tank top up over my head. Then he held my breasts in his hands.

"It's been a long time. Things could have changed."

"Not that." He massaged my breasts and began to kiss my neck.

I reached down and took his dick in my hands. As I massaged, he got more erect and I got more excited. "I need you inside of me."

"Lay back and let me get you ready." Zack slid his hands down my body, pushing my shorts down as he went. When I was on my back, he gripped my thighs and pulled me to the edge of the bed. He began to kiss my thighs as soon as he got down on his knees.

It didn't take long for Zack's lips to get reacquainted with my pussy. He ate like he was ending a fast and had me crying out in appreciation. My body was responding to him as if no time had passed. Zack hadn't forgotten how to make me cum. I arched my back and wrapped one leg over his shoulder while I rode the wave of my orgasm. I thought he was going to stop but he didn't. He just buried his face between my legs and kept going. My second orgasm took my breath away.

"You still with me, YaniBelle?" Zack asked in between planting kisses on my thigh. All I could do was nod. A few moments passed and Zack was massaging my thighs with his hands. "You ready for more?"

Before I could respond, he was easing his dick inside me. He had my legs in his arms and a firm grip on my ass.

"You feel so fucking good, YaniBelle."

I wanted to say something back but the only thing that escaped my lips was a moan. I gripped the blanket under me and tried to respond to each of his strokes. It felt so good it was hard to stay focused and not get lost in the feeling of bliss. Each stroke pushed me closer and closer to the edge until I climaxed again. I cried out until I lost my breath. Zack picked up the speed of his strokes and climaxed right after me.

I watched Zack through my blurry eyes. He took off the condom and headed for his bathroom. A few moments later he came back and sat down next to me. He leaned over and kissed me softly.

"You good?" He smiled at me.

"Wonderful." I nodded. "I need a nap."

“So, let’s take a nap then.” Zack scooted up to the top of the bed. I followed him and we got under the covers. He wrapped me in his arms. “Comfortable?”

“Yes.” I rested my head on the pillow and sighed. I closed my eyes and quickly drifted off to sleep.

I woke up to Zack kissing me on my forehead.

He smiled at me. “I ordered dinner. I hope you still like the things I remember you liking.”

“What did you get?”

“Chinese.”

I sat up. Zack traced his fingers down my neck. I moved his hand and smiled. “Stop that. We are supposed to be having dinner.”

"Okay."

"Where are my clothes?"

"You need those?"

"I'm not wandering around your place naked." I paused. "Especially while you're wearing clothes."

Zack went to take his shirt off and I stopped him. He chuckled, reached on the other side of him, and handed me my tank top and shorts. "Here you are."

"Thank you."

Zack stood up but didn't move away. He watched me get dressed. When I finished, I stood up and faced him. He leaned in and kissed me. "Let's eat."

We sat on the balcony just off his great room and ate. Instead of getting plates, we ate directly out of the containers like we used to. We passed containers back and forth.

“Tell me what you don’t tell social media.” Zack paused. “I know you don’t share even half of what goes on.”

I laughed. “Not even a quarter.”

“So, fill me in.”

“You want twenty years’ worth of information in one evening?”

“Nope. We’ve got all week. I just want to get started.”

“Okay. As long as you talk too.”

“We’ll take turns.” Zack gently nudged me. “Just random stuff.”

We started taking turns telling each other whatever random things that we could think of. Mostly we talked about things we did for fun. The rest of our evening was filled with stories of weekend trips and longer vacations. We cleaned up from dinner and sat back out on the balcony to enjoy the evening. I was comfortable with my legs across his lap. We sat out there for a good little while. Then, when it was pretty late, we headed inside and got back in his bed. We talked until I drifted off to sleep in his arms.

Sleeping in felt so good. I woke up at my usual early hour but Zack was still asleep with his arms around me. After just a few moments of being awake, his deep breathing lulled me back to sleep. When I woke up again, Zack was sitting up next to me. He was gently running his fingers down my cheek.

"Is it still morning?" I asked.

He smiled. "Yes."

"Good morning."

"Good morning." He leaned down and kissed me. "I'm taking you to brunch."

“That sounds nice.” I sat up. “I guess that means I should get up and get ready.”

“I’m not rushing you.” Zack kissed my bare shoulder.

“But my stomach is.”

Zack chuckled. “So, I guess I’ll let you get up and get ready then.”

I got up and slipped on my slippers. I smiled as Zack’s finger grazed my bare thigh as I walked past him. “I won’t be long.”

“Take your time. I might come and watch.”

The memory of when Zack used to watch me get ready had me smiling all the way to the guest bedroom. He always used to make me feel like I was putting on a show even when I wasn’t doing anything other than my normal routine. He could never watch me take a shower without getting involved but every other part of getting ready was a spectator sport for him. So, I wasn't shocked when I came out of the guest room bathroom after my shower and Zack was sitting on the guest bed. He was in a burgundy short sleeve shirt that showed off his nice build and a pair of dark gray pants.

"Did I miss you putting on lotion?" He frowned.

"Yes."

"Damn."

"You look nice."

"Thank you. Not as nice as you though." He smiled.

I looked down at my body wrapped in a towel. Then I looked up at him. "You have nice towels."

"Glad you like them."

I walked over to my suitcase and picked out a bra and panty set to put on. Zack started humming when I put my panties on and that caused me to giggle. I got my bra on and got it comfortable, and then walked over to the closet. It was an easy decision to pick my black sundress. I wanted to wear a dress and only had four to choose from. One was purple and would clash with Zack's shirt. The other was a t-shirt dress and felt too casual. The last one was a bit too dressy. I brought it just in case. Since Zack promised to wear a suit again, I decided to save it for that. After pulling my dress on, I walked back over to my suitcase and pulled out a pair of sandals.

"I like those."

"They're cute and comfortable." I sat next to him and put my sandals on.

Zack slipped his arms around my waist and kissed me on my cheek. "What's left because you look beautiful?"

“Light makeup and I gotta fix my braids.” I turned and met his lips with mine.

“You never used to wear makeup.”

“I like to do my eyes and put a little color on my lips.” I kissed him again and then stood up. “Ten minutes.”

He stood up. “Okay. I’m going to make a call.”

“Okay.” I grabbed my makeup bag and went into the bathroom. I pulled my braids up into a neat bun, switched my earrings, and then went to work on my eyes. Five minutes later Zack was leaning in the doorway. I smiled at his reflection in the mirror. Then I did my lip liner and lipstick. Once I was finished, I turned to face him. “I’m ready. I just need to grab my purse.”

Zack nodded and led the way. I grabbed my smaller purse and quickly tossed a few things in it from the larger one I carried on the plane. Then I caught up to Zack who was waiting by the door.

The restaurant was only about fifteen minutes from Zack's place. When we arrived, they seemed to be expecting us and seated us right away. We were inside, but next to a window with a beautiful view of the water. Our waiter came over a few moments after we were seated.

Zack looked at me. "They have a great peach sangria. Or would you like mimosa?"

"The sangria sounds lovely." I looked over the menu. Every so often I would look up and notice Zack looking at me. I tried to focus on figuring out what I was going to eat but I couldn't. "You already know what you want?"

"Yes."

"So, you are just going to stare at me?"

"I can't help it."

“Look at your phone.”

He smiled. “It will distract me from the view.”

We held eye contact for a few moments before I put the menu down. “What should I order?”

“They make wonderful omelets. Honestly, everything I’ve had here is good. You might like the shrimp and grits.”

“What are you getting?”

“Steak and eggs.”

I nodded and then looked over the menu one more time. The waiter came back and sat a pitcher of sangria on the table and an empty glass in front of each of us. He poured us each a glass before asking if we were ready to order. I ordered an omelet and, when Zack promised to share with me, the shrimp and grits. Zack ordered his food and then looked at me after the waiter left.

I sipped my sangria. “This is good.”

Zack took a sip, never taking his eyes off of me.

“What’s on your mind?” I smiled at him.

“You.”

“What about me?”

“How has someone not married you yet?”

I thought for a moment. “No one has met up to my high standards.”

“That’s my girl. Demand your worth.”

“What about you?”

He was quiet for a few moments before answering. “I haven’t been interested in it. Other things have had my attention.”

“Like what?”

“Work, mostly.”

“Tell me about your work.” I sat back in my chair and sipped my drink.

Zack sat back and told me about leaving Atlanta, where we met, to come to Miami. “It wasn’t the same without you.”

I raised an eyebrow. “Really?”

He chuckled. “That was part of it.”

“A small part.”

“A sizable part.” Zack winked at me. Then he went on to tell me about getting the opportunity to transfer locations with the warehouse he worked for. Once he got to Miami, he connected with a friend from high school and got into real estate. Things went up from there. “I found that I am really good at it.”

“So, you sell houses?”

“I buy and sell property. It’s mostly commercial real estate at this point but every now and again I get into residential flipping."

"I just bought my first place a few years ago." The waiter sat our food down on the table. I moved the large bowl of shrimp and grits to the middle of the table so we both could reach it.

"My condo is the fifth one I've owned just for myself. I was an initial investor when the building was being built."

"So, you move a lot?"

"No." Zack shook his head. "I hate moving."

I laughed. "Oh."

"I've been in this place for five years. I don't see myself moving again for a little while longer." He paused. "I'd eventually like to settle down on an island somewhere."

"That sounds nice." I smiled. "I remember you always used to talk about living on an island."

"Now that I have been to more of them, I'm convinced that it needs to happen."

"Part of your retirement plan."

"I don't think I'll ever retire." He smiled. "I'll just work less."

"I plan on retiring."

"I remember you saying your job is stressful." He shook his head. "I mentor but I couldn't imagine working with kids full time."

"It isn't for everybody."

"Me. I am everybody."

I covered my mouth as I laughed while chewing food.

"How long have you been doing it?"

"Fifteen years."

"Wow."

"The past five years have been with middle schoolers. I've worked with other age groups and I find this to be the most challenging."

"Puberty. So much about their lives is changing. Then getting ready for high school." Zack shook his head. "Nope."

"Is that why you haven't had kids?"

"I'm barely taking care of myself."

"I think you are doing a good job of taking care of yourself."

"My friends remind me to take vacations because I wouldn't otherwise."

I smiled. "I like the freedom of only having to worry about myself."

"Feeding myself is a chore. I can't imagine needing to feed someone else."

"Wine and cookies have been dinner many a night."

"Rum and cake."

"We need to do better."

"Maybe you'll retire and come down here so we can take care of each other." He raised an eyebrow at me.

I quietly ate a bite of my food and looked out at the view. "How do you get anything done being so close to the beach?"

"I walk on the beach at least a few times a week."

"Really?"

"Mostly at sunrise but I come out in the evenings every so often. I've been known to work from the beach every once and a while."

"Seems like a really relaxed life."

"Hardly." Zack chuckled. "It's a balance."

"I understand. I have to make sure I do things I enjoy on my time off because otherwise I would go insane." I paused. "The last few weeks at work have been rough."

"You have been posting hints of that so I'm glad you've come down to relax."

"Have I? I try not to post about work."

"I've only been following you on social media and online for like twenty years. I can tell. You're stressed."

I smiled at him. "We met online ages ago."

"The first girl I met in person." He smiled at me. "By far the best."

"The best?"

"Yes. To this day." Zack laughed. "My luck with online meetings and dating apps sucks."

“It has been hit or miss for me.”

“How did you meet the guy who I at least owe a drink to?”

I laughed. “A drink?”

“Yes. Taking a break from you requires a drink. Gonna need something when you realize how big of an idiot you are.”

“You know from experience?”

“Exactly.” Zack smiled.

“I met him at a happy hour.”

“How long have y’all been together?”

I sipped my sangria. “A little over a year.”

Zack shook his head. “I’m thankful for his stupidity.”

“He’s been texting me and leaving voicemail messages for a few days now.”

“Didn’t take him long to figure out he was stupid.”

"I'll respond eventually." I paused. "When I get home."

"Maybe."

I smiled at him. "Maybe."

"I should have followed you when you left Atlanta."

"Then you wouldn't be where you are today. Everything happens for a reason." I put a shrimp in my mouth. I wanted to say more but didn't. There were several times over the years I wondered what would have happened if Zack and I had decided to get serious and stay together.

"Maybe you're right."

"Maybe." I smiled at him.

After brunch, we ended up back at Zack's condo and in his bed. We had dinner on his balcony again and then ended up enjoying a bath together. The next morning, we sat on the balcony outside his bedroom and watched the sunrise before he had me holding onto the railing as he employed a few different techniques to make me climax. Zack had not forgotten how to please me. Every single thing he tried worked. I was glad that he still responded to me the way he used to. With all the time that had passed, nothing had changed in that regard. We spent that whole day having sex and taking naps curled up together.

The next day, we got up early and went to the beach to watch the sunrise. It was breathtaking to sit and watch the sky and the waves. We didn't talk the entire time. Afterward, we grabbed breakfast and headed back to the condo to get ready for the day.

"We are going out today. I can't keep you in bed all week, as much as I would like to." Zack winked at me.

Zack drove us to an area called Wynwood. It was a wonderful arts district. We walked around looking at art installations, going to galleries, shopping, and eating. Zack insisted on buying me anything I wanted. I took so many pictures of the wonderful art. The graffiti walls were my favorite. Zack took a few pictures of me in front of certain pieces. I got him to pose for one picture with me. He didn't like being in pictures.

"I don't know how you have pictures up on your socials."

"Most were taken against my will or without my knowledge. Every once in a while, I actually pose."

"You posed for me at the airport."

"You're different."

I laughed.

"How are you going to choose which ones to post? You've taken a hundred."

"I'll scroll through and pick my favorites. I'm not posting anything until I get back home."

"I usually post pictures weeks after they are taken."

"I don't want people too much in my business."

"Exactly."

We had a wonderful day out. I even snuck a few pictures of Zack while he wasn't paying attention. There were a lot of people out but it wasn't overly crowded. My legs were so tired by the end of it.

Zack glanced at me at the red light. "So, we'll have another soak in the tub tonight?"

I smiled at him. "An actual soak."

"Then a massage."

"You just want to touch me."

"Of course." He winked at me before focusing back on the road.

I reached over and rested my hand on his thigh. "It's okay. I wanna touch you too."

Zack made me eggs for breakfast the next morning while I leaned against the counter wearing only his t-shirt. It was good to see he still remembered what I taught him. We caught each other up on how our families were doing. It started with him asking about my mother. He had met her a few times when she came to visit me in Atlanta. Then it grew into all the people we used to tell each other about.

“You know my mother still asks about you.” He said before eating a bite of his eggs. We were still standing at the counter.

“She only met me once.”

“You made a great impression.”

I smiled. Zack used to always go home to see his mom. She came to visit him one time. It was a surprise visit and I happened to be at his place when she popped up. I was going to leave but she insisted I stay. I insisted on making dinner for everyone since she had been on the road for a few hours. I went back to my dorm room after dinner and left them to enjoy the weekend together. After that, Zack said she always asked about me whenever they talked.

“She was very upset with me for letting you go.”

“Did you tell her we both agreed it was for the best?”

“She didn’t care.”

“Was she like this with all your girlfriends?”

“No.”

I sighed. “Tell her I said hi.”

“I’m not telling her you were here. She’ll kill me for letting you go back home.”

“She won’t.” I laughed.

“If my sister didn’t have kids, I think she would have disowned me.”

I held my side laughing. When I finally collected myself, I looked at him. “My mother was disappointed that we didn’t get married but she let it go.”

“My mother doesn’t let anything go.”

“I’m sorry.”

“So now I have to get you to move down here to make her happy.”

“Her happy?”

"Me too."

I ate the last of my eggs and didn't respond. We were quiet for a bit. Zack put the dishes in the dishwasher. Then he looked at me. I ran my fingers down his arm. "What's on the agenda for today?"

"Movies in bed. Dinner out later." Zack played with the hem of the shirt I was wearing.

"I like the sound of that."

"I want to make sure you're relaxing." He took my hand and led me out of the kitchen. "You get to pick the movies."

"What if I pick something you don't like?"

"Then I'll busy myself distracting you."

I laughed. "You really haven't changed at all."

Zack looked back at me and winked.

It was actually chilly the next morning. I still insisted we go to the beach since we were both awake. I wore the jacket I had for when I returned home to cooler weather. Zack took me to a different area than we had been before. It was just us for as far as I could see. I stayed in the grass for a bit and watched Zack stand closer to the water and watch the sun. He looked deep in thought and I wondered what was on his mind. There were only a few more days left in my trip and I knew it was going to be hard for me to leave. The day before had been the most relaxing day, in bed watching movies. We went to dinner in Coconut Grove and there was a live band. Then we went back to his condo and took a shower together where I learned that Zack could still hold me up in the air for an extended period of time.

Zack looked back at me and smiled. I smiled and got up from where I was sitting. He met me halfway and took my hands in his.

“You okay?”

I nodded. “Yes.”

“Wanna walk a little bit?”

“Sure.”

We held hands and walked down the beach slowly. I felt more relaxed than I had been in a long time. I really wanted to bottle that feeling and save it for future moments when I needed it. I hoped the memory of it would be enough.

After our walk on the beach, we had breakfast at a cute little cafe. Then we went back to the condo. I didn't realize I was sleepy until I sat on the couch and immediately dozed off. I felt like I had only blinked when Zack was kissing me on my forehead.

"Sorry to interrupt your nap."

"I was asleep?"

"Yes. For about twenty minutes."

"Oh."

"I have an issue at the office and have to go in."

I nodded and sat up. "Okay. I'll be fine."

"I shouldn't be gone more than a couple of hours."

"Okay." I stretched my arms above my head. "I might finish that nap I didn't know I needed."

Zack kissed me softly. "Call or text me if you need anything while I'm gone."

"I will."

He kissed me again before heading to the door. I watched him leave and then rested my head back on the couch. After a few moments with my eyes closed, I sighed. I opened my eyes and got up. First stop was the kitchen. I got a glass of lemonade. Then I went and grabbed my tablet from my bag. Next stop was the balcony. I got comfortable on the outdoor sofa and started reading. The weather had warmed up and there was a really nice breeze blowing. I barely got a few chapters in before I dozed off.

I woke up hot and sweaty. The temperature had risen pretty fast. I checked my phone and saw that Zack had sent me a text to check up on me. I sent him one back saying I had just woken up and was fine. Then I gathered my things and went inside. I went into the guest room and sat my things down. I decided to take a long shower and enjoy the amazing water pressure in Zack's shower. I left my clothes and toiletry bag on Zack's bed. The only thing I took in the bathroom with me was my shower gel. The warm water of his shower massaged my body and helped me to relax even more than I already was.

Zack startled me when he stood in the doorway to the bathroom. I hadn't shut the door. He smiled at me. "Didn't mean to scare you."

I turned the water off. "It's okay."

He grabbed a towel and wrapped me in it when I stepped out of the shower. "That took longer than I wanted it to."

"I don't think it took long at all. I read a little, took a nap, and had a nice shower." I leaned forward and kissed him. "Did everything go okay?"

"Yeah. Things are back on track."

"Good."

“From the looks of the clothes on my bed, you want to stay in for the rest of the day.”

“Did you have plans?”

“I always have something up my sleeve just in case.” He kissed me. “But I would rather just chill with you.”

“So, let’s just chill.” I smiled. “What do you have that we can cook for dinner?”

“If I don’t have what you want, I’ll go to the store and get it.” Zack held me tight in his arms.

“You gotta let me get dressed so I can see what you are working with.”

“You already know what I’m working with.”

I pushed him gently and laughed. “In your fridge.”

“Oh. My mind was already elsewhere.”

“I see that.” I broke free of his hold. “You get into some comfortable clothes. I’m going to explore your kitchen.”

“I guess I’ll shower alone.” He frowned.

“I’ll wrinkle up if I get back in.” I sat on his bed and pulled out my lotion. Zack stood and watched me. I glanced up at him. “I thought you were going to shower.”

“When I come back from the store.”

“You might not have to go.”

He chuckled. “I know what’s in my fridge.”

After I got dressed, we headed to his kitchen. I could tell he really didn’t cook. I pulled out an ice cream bar from his freezer and looked at him while I opened it. “You really don’t cook at all.”

“Only when I’m in the mood.” He smiled. “I’m just rarely in the mood.”

“So, you just want to order out tonight?”

"No. I want to cook with you." He had a pad of paper and a pen in his hand. He leaned against the counter, ready to write. "What am I getting from the store?"

I gave him the list in between bites of the ice cream bar. I was almost finished the list when I noticed him paying more attention to me and the ice cream rather than writing things down. "Zack!"

"Huh?"

"Focus."

"I am."

"On the list." I licked the ice cream that was starting to melt down my hand and smiled. "Focus on the list."

"I'd rather focus on your lips."

I kissed him. "After dinner, these lips will focus on you. How about that?"

"I like the sound of that." He grinned.

I took the paper and pen from him and finished writing down the items he missed. “You want me to go with you?”

“Naw. I’m good. You stay here and relax.” Zack took the list, kissed me on the forehead, and then headed for the door.

Zack was gone for about thirty minutes. I sat on the couch and read a few more chapters while I waited. When he got home, I got everything set up for us to cook while he took a shower. For someone who didn’t cook, he had all the right pots and pans. I knew that his mother probably had something to do with that. Especially when I saw the cast iron griddle. Once he was back in the kitchen, we got started with dinner. Zack had me sit on a stool on the other side of the kitchen counter and give instructions while he did all the cooking. He did let me cut a few things to help but he did most of it. I was pleasantly surprised that he owned a rice cooker.

“I cook rice a lot when I do cook.” He pulled the appliance out of the cabinet and rinsed the rice.

“Put some minced onion and salt in there with the rice.”

He raised an eyebrow at me. “I don’t usually add anything but rice and water.”

“It’ll be good. I promise.” I smiled. “Use the onions from your spice cabinet.”

Once he got the rice going, he checked the griddle pan that I told him to heat up. “Is this too hot?”

“Nope. It’s perfect. Add some more oil and then put the chicken on.” I paused. “Are you going to remember all this or should I be writing this down for you?”

“I’ll remember.” He paused. “And if I forget I’ll just call you.”

I laughed. “I have a feeling you’d call me whether you remembered or not.”

"You're right."

I remembered back when I first moved away from Atlanta. Zack and I talked a lot on the phone for the first few months. Then I got busy with work and grad school. He was always busy but made time when he could. I couldn't exactly remember when it fell off completely but it did. We got to the point where we only communicated on social media.

"I'm going to call and text and private message you until you get sick of me."

Our eyes met and I smiled at him. "Good."

It rained all day the next day. Zack and I had no problem camping out in his living room and watching movies all day. We napped together, which was really nice.

Zack ordered takeout for both lunch and dinner. It was late when we headed back to his bedroom.

I turned to him. “Tomorrow is my last full day here.”

Zack pouted. “Don’t remind me.”

“What are we going to do?”

“Probably sleep in.”

I yawned and nodded. “Probably.”

“I’m taking you to dinner and a show tomorrow night.”

“You gonna wear the suit like you promised?”

“Yes.”

“I’m excited.” I sat down on the bed.

“Are you?”

I nodded. Then I yawned. “I’ll be even more excited tomorrow.”

"Let's go to bed."

We got in bed and Zack immediately held me in his arms. I was so comfortable. As I drifted off to sleep, I knew I was going to miss that feeling.

Dinner was amazing and the concert was great but I spent the whole night wanting to get Zack out of that suit I asked him to wear. It was clearly tailored to fit him and he looked amazing in it. He watched me get dressed again and it took longer than usual because I couldn't stop looking at him and he kept wanting to help me. He held my hand on the ride to our destinations. On the ride home, he rested his free hand on the part of my thigh that was open through the split in my dress. I had to resist the urge to move his hand a bit higher. When we walked from the car to the condo, Zack kept his hand on the small of my back. My dress was open in the back all the way down to the top of my ass. He had his hand right there, with a few fingers under the fabric.

When we got inside the condo, Zack pulled me back and pinned me to the closed door. We looked each other in the eye for a moment before he leaned his head down and kissed me on my neck. I pushed his jacket off his shoulders while his hands moved up the two splits in my dress. He took the jacket off and let it fall to the ground. Then he lifted my dress up at the splits. Zack grabbed my thighs and led me over to the couch. I reached down and undid his pants while he pulled my panties down off my ass. After I stepped out of them, I pushed Zack down on the couch. He reached into the splits of my dress and grabbed me by my thighs again. He gently pulled me closer.

“Come down here with me.”

I got down on his lap. Zack pushed the bottom of my dress up and out of his way. His fingers quickly slipped inside me while his thumb began to massage my clit. Our lips met and our tongues quickly began to tangle. I freed his dick and gripped him as we kissed. It didn't take long for him to finger fuck me to orgasm. He stopped kissing me long enough to lick his fingers and put a condom on. I lifted up so that he could ease inside of me. Then I began to ride him.

"Shit, YaniBelle." Zack moaned in between kisses all over my neck and the bare part of my chest.

I rode him through my second orgasm that had me closing my eyes and moaning his name. Once I was coherent again, I got up and turned around in his lap. Zack slipped right back inside of me and gripped my hips. I bent over and braced my hands on the floor for balance. I met each one of his strokes as he drove us both to the edge of bliss. His fingers found my clit and began to massage again to make sure that I climaxed when he did.

When we finished, I sat back up and Zack wrapped his arms around me tight. He planted kisses all over the back of my neck while we caught our breath. We got up a few minutes later and made our way to his bed, taking our clothes off before getting comfortable under the covers.

We were facing each other when he kissed me softly and looked into my eyes. "I know you have to leave tomorrow but I'm not letting you go. I'm going to have to come and visit you and try and convince you to come back to Miami."

I wasn't sure what to say so I simply kissed him and smiled. I really wanted him to do exactly what he said he would. I wasn't sure if it would work but I wanted him to try.

Charmaine got out of her car and gave me the once over. “You look like a well-rested woman.”

“Don’t joke. I slept on the plane. He had me up all night.”

She laughed as she opened her trunk. “You look stress-free.”

“It was a relaxing trip.” I put my suitcase in her trunk and stepped back.

“No trouble with him and you leaving?” She shut the trunk.

“He pouted the whole way to the airport.” I smiled remembering the sad look on his face. “I almost didn’t come back.”

“Enjoyed yourself that much. Nice.”

We both got in her car. I looked at her. “I didn’t think it would be that hard to leave but it felt harder than it was years ago.”

“Coming back to reality is hard.” She smiled at me and then pulled out into traffic.

I sighed. “He wants me to move down there with him. He said he would settle for me spending the summer with him. He also said he is coming to visit me in a few weeks.”

“Oh wow. So, this is going to be a thing.” She paused. “What about Mike?”

“Who?”

Char laughed. “Has he been in touch since being dumb?”

“Several missed calls, ignored voice mails, and unread text messages.”

“You haven’t even been curious?”

“Didn’t want to ruin my vibe.”

"And now that you are back home?"

"I'm no longer interested in someone who isn't sure about me. Maybe that changed for him but no matter what happens with Zack, I'm too old for that bullshit."

Char held her hand up and we high-fived. "I know that's right."

"I'm not going to let a week convince me that Zack is serious either. He's going to have to prove it to me."

"Good."

"This past week was wonderful and I just hope that he can keep it up."

"In more ways than one."

I swatted at her arm and laughed. "Stop it."

"You walked right into that one."

“I’m burnt out from work and could use a change but I also don’t want to jump at the first opportunity that presents itself.”

“You could find a job down there.” Char quickly glanced at me. “One that is a little less stressful.”

“I love working with kids. That is going to be stressful.”

“Well, one that is different from what you are doing now. I don’t understand how you can work with the age group you do.”

“Maybe I’ll work with high schoolers next.” I looked out the window. Then I turned back to Char. “You want me to move away?”

“If you move to Miami then I can come and visit.” She grinned.

“Ulterior motive.”

“Yup.”

My phone vibrated and I looked down to see I had a message from Zack. I sent him a quick text as soon as I got off the plane to let him know I landed safely. I checked the message and smiled. It was a screenshot of his flight confirmation to come and visit. "That was quick."

"What?"

"He is coming to visit."

"When?"

"In three weeks. He said he had a packed schedule but he made time."

"That's a start in the right direction."

I smiled. "Yes. Yes it is. Let's see where this goes."

"I'll make sure I have my popcorn. I love a good romance."

I laughed.

~THE END~

Other works by Turtleberry

Are You Okay?

Nobody's Somebody

Sweet Turtleberry Jam Volume One

These Women Book One

These Women Book Two

These Women Book Three

Happily Ever After

Sweet Turtleberry Jam Volume Two

Catching Evie

Needs To Be Met

Love Unexpected

Lena's Chance At Love

Both Sides Of Me

Whiskey Kisses

Halloween Spice

It For Me

Days of Summer

One More Kiss

The Friend

Finding Love

My Neighbor

www.ingramcontent.com/pod-product-compliance
Lightning Source LLC
LaVergne TN
LVHW050331160826
845677LV00014B/3596

* 9 7 9 8 8 4 8 8 0 9 5 2 7 *